For Tori   N.J.

For Eliana   C.R.

The Hello, Goodbye Window

Story by **Norton Juster**
Pictures by **Chris Raschka**

MICHAEL DI CAPUA BOOKS   **HYPERION BOOKS FOR CHILDREN**

Nanna and Poppy live in a big house
in the middle of town.
There's a brick path
that goes to the
back porch, but
before you get there
you pass right by
the kitchen window.

That's the Hello, Goodbye Window.
It looks like a regular window,
but it's not.

The kitchen is where Nanna and Poppy
are most of the time.
So you can climb up on the flower barrel
and tap the window,
then duck down and they won't know
who did it,
or you can press your face
against the glass and frighten them.
If they're not in the kitchen, you can't do
any of those things and you have to wait
until next time.

If they see you first,
they wave and make silly faces.
Sometimes Nanna peek-a-boos me,
which always makes me laugh.
So I get a lot of extra fun and hellos
before I even get inside.

Just look at the kitchen. It's so big. It has a table you can color on and lots of drawers to take stuff out of and play with.
But you can't touch anything under the sink.
You could get very sick.

There are shelves full of glass jars with lots of everything in them, a step stool so I can wash my hands, and all kinds of pictures from the olden days. Nanna says she even used to give me a bath in the sink when I was little—really!

Sometimes Poppy plays his harmonica for me.
He can only play one song, "Oh, Susannah."
But he can play it a lot of different ways.
He can play it slow or fast

or he can play it sitting down or standing up.
He says he can even play it and
drink a glass of water at the same time,
but I've never seen him do that.

When I stay over we have our supper in the kitchen too
and when it's dark outside
we can look at our reflections in the window.
It works just like a mirror
except it's not in the bathroom,
and it looks like we're outside
looking in.
Poppy says,
"What are you doing out there?
You come right in and have your dinner."

And I say, "But I'm here with you, Poppy,"
and then he looks at me
in his funny way.

Just before I go up to bed, Nanna turns off
all the lights and we stand by the window
and say good night to the stars.

Do you know how many stars there are?
Neither do I, but she knows them all.

In the morning the first place we go is back to the kitchen, and there's the window waiting for us. You can look out and say good morning to the garden or see if it's going to rain or be nice.

In the morning the first place we go is back to the
kitchen, and there's the window waiting for us.
You can look out and say good morning to the garden
or see if it's going to rain or be nice.

Do you know how many stars there are?
Neither do I, but she knows them all.

And you can see if the dog next door is doing stuff in Nanna's flower beds. She hates that!

Sometimes Poppy says in a real loud voice,
"HELLO, WORLD! WHAT HAVE YOU GOT FOR US TODAY?"
Nobody ever answers, but he doesn't care.

Poppy makes breakfast.
He says it's his specialty.

My favorite is oatmeal
with bananas and raisins
that you can't see
because he hides them
down inside.

I find them all.

When I get dressed, I help Nanna in the garden.
It's a very nice garden, but there's a tiger
who lives behind the big bush in the back
so I don't ever go there.

I ride my bike too.
"Not in the street, please."

Or collect sticks and acorns.
"Not in the house, please."

Then sometimes I just sit by the Hello, Goodbye Window
and watch. Nanna says it's a magic window
and anybody can come along when you least expect it.

TYRANNOSAURUS REX

(He's extinct, so he doesn't come around much.)

THE PIZZA DELIVERY GUY
(Pepperoni and cheese, he knows that's my favorite.)

THE QUEEN OF ENGLAND
(Nanna is English, you know,
so the Queen likes
to come for tea.)

They all could come! And a lot more if they want!
And if they do, I'll see them first.

Mommy and Daddy pick me up after work.
I'm glad because I know we're going home,
but it makes me sad too because I have to leave
Nanna and Poppy.
You can be happy and sad
at the same time, you know.
It just happens that way sometimes.

When we leave we always stop at the window
to blow kisses goodbye.

When you look from the outside,
Nanna and Poppy's house has lots of windows,
but there's only one Hello, Goodbye Window
and it's right where you need it.

When I get my own house someday
I'm going to have a special
Hello, Goodbye Window too.
By that time I might be a Nanna myself.
I don't know who the Poppy will be,
but I hope he can play the harmonica.